STREET FACTS

A THRILLER ILLUMINATING DARKER MYSTERIOUS SIDES OF STREETS

SANHITA MUKHERJEE

Made with ♥ on the Notion Press Platform
www.notionpress.com

The Readers

Contents

CHAPTER ONE

Fact Struck

The streets were getting ready for the upcoming Independence Day Parade. It meant lots of traffic detours till a week after fifteenth. Especially, local passenger buses were especially not allowed along the route of parade and tableaux.

Shreeja had to get down at PG hospital stoppage, instead of her usual stoppage at Park Street. The latter used to be within walking distance from her office at Bishwaniketan building. The former was not too far either. She decided to walk; hence, crossed the roads, then kept walking along western boundary of Rabindrasadan, on footpaths. After ten feet of walk she, almost, stumbled upon a crawling child.

Without any thought, Shreeja picked up the baby. It was a boy. He was cooing. Looking at the curious round eyes, saliva smudged chin, Shreeja was touched by the natural joy of holding a baby. Before her feelings could even sink in, the baby pulled her glasses by the temples. She burst into laughter.

The baby was disappointed. He could not yank the glasses from Shreeja's ears and nose and lick to taste.

Then he concentrated on the pendant on Shreeja's necklace. He tried to pull it up, holding in his tiny left palm, right arm being around Shreeja's neck. The length of the necklace was insufficient for his purpose. So, he ducked down a little bit to put the pendant into his mouth and get a taste of the bright, pink and green object. Shreeja laughed louder.

One of the two women lying down, and probably sleeping on the footpath, suddenly sprang to her feet and charged at Shreeja, "What are you doing with the baby?"

Shreeja sensed the tension. She had been in a profession involving street encounters for nearly a decade. She had handled street junkies, random rapists, gang bangers on some of the most troubled corners of the city. She was accustomed to street arrogance and atrocities.

Since she was neither law enforcement nor rival street business, she pretended to be affable. She replied with a smile, "He was crawling towards the traffic. I was about to step on him. Somehow he managed to catch my attention. Now we're getting acquainted...."

The woman sighed, seemed relieved. She confessed, "I was not supposed to fall asleep. But the sultry weather..., slow business... Thanks for catching the baby. Otherwise they would have charged me with five hundred rupees for losing the child ..."

Shreeja's senses were shaken. Her jaws dropped. She considered herself a veteran of street affairs. She knew that no beggar happened just to be a beggar, but a drug peddler or gang informer. She never touched live mother and child sculptures on the streets, though. They seemed too sacred, a manifestation of subaltern haplessness. She could not help but utter, "Oh! He's not your son..... You're not his mother...."

The woman further clarified, "Nope. This' a begging fixture from dozens kept at my employer's warehouse.

Today I's asked to hold this baby and beg at this corner of the street. Yesterday, I's cleaning pots for a street food vendor. I asked today for a street food vending spot for myself. So, they asked me to prove my salesmanship through begging by paying them three hundred rupees daily, by the end of business day. If I'm satisfied by the end of the week about what I make without complaining about their share, then they may give me a street vending spot."

Shreeja's journalistic instinct aroused. She asked with a clever smile, "By yesterday, you didn't mean exactly the day before today?"

The woman nodded affirmatively. Shreeja asked again, "How long have you been working in this spot as a beggar?"

The woman's face was a mix of sadness and satisfaction. She shared with reservation, "Months. Before you ask anything further, I'm telling you I'm making enough for myself."

Now Shreeja frowned, "Yet your employer is not giving you a street vending spot...."

The woman confided, "What I've heard is that my employer thinks I'm a liar since I've not complained of what I make. Or, I'm an informer to competitions or the police."

Shreeja reflected sympathetically, "It happens in every job. Disgruntled employees chatter a lot about their mistreatment in the hands of peers, superiors, even if, issues were that these employees never complain..."

The woman smiled mischievously, "Oh. you naughty woman.. You meant that I'm complaining. Then let me tell you about misogyny in our profession. All street food vending spots are assigned only to men. Women are employed as cleaners. Not even as servers. Though we women are eternal household cooks and bookkeepers."

Shreeja did not pretend but teased directly this time, "And your husband beats you up every day, snatches your money, drinks hooch and doesn't care about feeding the children, not to mention raising them by engaging them in learning a trade or sending them to public schools..."

The woman took a stance of adding some more spice, "Until he left us for my satin. A homewrecker, bitch."

Shreeja handed the boy to the woman. Then she fished out a hundred rupees bill and another fifty rupees bill from purse. She handed the woman the fifty rupees and tucked the other bill in the fists of the boy.

The woman mentioned, "Thanks. But before you go you must know that my husband is a loving person. He used to be a hawker on local trains to Lakshmikantapur. Until he lost both his legs by falling from a moving train. He supports our children by sewing comforters from rags, making paper bags, and other odd jobs that do not need legs to move. I could have taken up his job at local trains. But our children were scared. My son goes to school and learns tailoring at a neighborhood shop. Daughter is attending school and learning by working at a beauty parlor."

Shreeja let a few moments pass before she reacted, "Truth?"

The women seemed crafty, "Maybe."

Shreeja handed her another hundred rupees bill and asked, "Give me the fifty back."

The woman did and reflected bitterness, "Thanks. But no thanks."

Shreeja bargained, "You can keep the fifty if we, you, the baby and me can have a selfie."

The woman agreed.

While walking towards her office, Shreeja felt an urgent need to smoke. She was pacing fast, suffocated by the shock that a child was worthy of only five hundred rupees.

CHAPTER TWO

Fact Search Stymied

Office was usually cacophonous. Everyone was trying to win by pulling strings on the others. So did Shreeja. She was competing to earn a name from ongoing rape stories. Being a woman, she had leverage. Whatever she uttered about men appeared to be authentic.

Her colleague Saurabh was at a spitting contest with her. He was there to save all men from the disgrace of a few perpetrators. He was shouting against misogyny, too. But he was always bringing the phrase "some men". The phrase was spoiling the continuum in the narrative that Shreeja was trying to build with a robust male hating rape fearing force, especially comprising gullible college and university students. Her goal was to turn every incident of groping, anus pricking, genital flashing, semen spilling by men at public spaces, in transits, as heinous as rape.

Throughout the evening, Shreeja felt distracted, every now and then, while interacting with college kids. Every boy she hushed up, irrespective of speaking for or against the motion she had created to prove all males being misogynous, reminded her of the boy she met late afternoon by the western walls of Rabindrasadan. A beautiful creature. Sadly, worth only five hundred rupees.

Her story that night turned out vastly different from previous ones. It was not a superficial slur putting all males in an offender box. It was rather insightful. It was about how boys used to be objectified since birth. It was about how objectifying every person around used to become a boy's normal activity and notion, how such notion could have created sex predators in society. Quoting psychiatry here and there.

Moumita, Sheeja's editor, called Shreeja in her cubicle. She exclaimed, "Is this your competition with Saurabh.... like debating... clinging to your side of notion!"

Shreeja felt disempowered by emotions. She needed some drinks, probably a joint, too. She could not argue her point properly, "I thought this was a natural balancing act. Instead of ..."

Moumita chopped her explanation, "The portal and the paper maintain balance. By you on one side, by Saurabh on the other. It's your job to disturb the balance by putting more weight on your side. Thus, the ball rolls here, the game goes on. Now if you start playing for Saurabh ... "

Moumita could not finish. Editor-in-chief, Tapaja, appeared in her cubicle. Obviously, she took the reign, "Why Shreeja's story is still on edit? Pagination team is waiting."

Moumita replied, "Shreeja's bombed tonight."

Tapaja was impatient, "What do you mean?"

Moumita explained, "Shreeja has changed sides. Yet she's no firepower."

Tapaja seemed intrigued, "Show me the piece."

Moumita left her chair. Tapaja started scanning on Moumita's computer screen. She finished in three minutes and pronounced her verdict, "OK. Good piece. It's not only way out of line, but almost on the other side."

She paused for a moment, then added, "The thing between Shreeja and Saurabh has been organic. Assume that Shreeja has changed her game. She has taken some unprecedented moves. That may dissatisfy her regular readers. But that would catch Saurabh's readers to her piece. Saurabh must react tomorrow on this. Let him know. Then, Shreeja would focus more on police procedure, for the remainder of the week. She can turn back to opinion-oriented pieces if we decide on weekly meetings, with readership figures."

Muomita clarified, "Hence, Shreeja's piece stays."

Tapaja confirms, "For a change."

Then she asks, "Shreeja, are your assignments clear for the week?"

Shreeja confirmed, "Yes, Tapaja di."

Later in the watering hole Saurabh caught Shreeja, "Hey! You piece of shit. You just pushed bamboo on my ass."

Shreeja asked, "Do you have a piece of joint? I don't have any..."

Saurabh asked back, "What's happened?"

Shreeja tried to laugh, "Nothing. Just..."

Saurabh insisted, "We're partners in this. Even if you don't share why your whole being has changed, I still can sense. I know for sure that you're topsy-turvy."

After a while, Shreeja turned completely drunk, started booze talking, "Who does rent children? Only for five hundred rupees? Who employs beggars?"

Saurabh was listening. He responded, "Let's get those motherfuckers."

Shreeja seconded, "Let's do that."

Saurabh asked, "Tomorrow?"

Shreeja stood up from the barstool, "Not tomorrow. Wait..."

She ran to the washroom. Puked. Smudged her long hair and parts of her shirt with vomit. Splashed some water to clean up, got drenched. Yet she cleaned herself up.

She returned to the barstool. Paid for her drinks. Touched Saurabh's shoulder. Saurabh raised his left eyebrow as if asking, "Hence?"

Shreeja replied, "From tomorrow I'm pursuing police procedure of the rape spree."

Saurabh responded, "Good to know. After shitting on your today's shit, I'll pursue the offenders then."

Shreeja felt relieved, "Then we'll be back in our respective games with changed dimensions but same paradigm."

Saurabh changed his tone, "What about the beggars bugging you?"

Shreeja's face darkened, "I'll start with police station tomorrow."

Saurabh finished his drink, paid and concluded, "Tomorrow I'll be busy shitting on your shit. So, I won't be there with you tomorrow. But I would really appreciate it if you let me into the beggars' shit."

Shreeja went back to office to collect her staff and board an office drop-off vehicle with morning newspapers. She stopped riding cabs during late nights, wee hours, after the rape spree shook the city.

CHAPTER THREE

Fact from the Police

Next afternoon Shreeja woke up sober. Her pillow and neck were wet, though the air conditioner was working fine. Her eyes were swollen. She felt as if she had wept her heart out. Her recollection of the day before brought her bitterness and grief back.

Rushing downstairs, she felt lighter. She was glad that she was not hung over. Scanning through the morning newspaper, she pointed to Saurabh's piece. It was good. Reluctantly she went through her piece. She found that Moumita added a few twists to blame misogyny and kept the tone of the series intact. But it did not excite Shreeja anymore. She texted Saurabh, "You SoB, up by one score."

She took shower, got dressed, ate lunch, called a cab to arrive at Park Street Police Station.

The police station, too, was under the spell of Independence Day celebration and related security preparations. It was totally distracted from rape cases. Shreeja waited for the duty officer to allot her a desk. It took more than a quarter of an hour.

The sub-inspector at the desk was a woman. Her name was Manidipa Mitra. Shreeja was direct, "Ms. Mitra, I'm here to take note on status of the rape cases."

Young and enthusiastic Ms. Mitra replied, "Oh! a lot has been going on. As you know the accused persons are in police remand."

She stopped there. Shreeja waited for some more spunky frivolity. But nothing other than silence emanated. Shreeja asked, "What's new?"

Sub-inspector Mitra replied, "Several things."

She paused and shared, as if confiding, "Can't share. This' an ongoing investigation."

Shreeja enquired, "Are you the investigating officer?"

Monidipa Mitra replied, "No. A task force of senior detectives and police persons are pursuing the cases. I'm representing this police station among other stations involved in the case."

Shreeja got a notch to scratch, "Are everyone in the team women?"

Monidipa Mitra appeared clever, "We don't encourage gender bias in the department. Is there anything else I can help you with?"

Shreeja expressed dissatisfaction, "You've not shared any useful information at all. Ma'am your youth and enthusiasm seem false for you're guarding important public information from the public you serve."

Manidipa mustered up a bitchy smile and responded, "I'm at your service, madam. Please don't call me ma'am. My colleagues call me Mitra. You can call me Mitra, too. Also, you should understand that my duties are to the public but not to corporates in the news business. My job is to save people from criminals, even risking my own life. It's not to save your job. Also, speaking of information, you can lodge an information request under RTI act at Lalbazar."

Shreeja thought she had wasted much of her day. She headed for a notary office to buy a few stamp papers each worth rupees ten. Then she headed back to office to type her enquiries, on those stamp papers, as prescribed under the Right to Information Act. One for her assignment on rape spree. The other was on the beggars. She submitted them at the city police commissioner's office at Lalbazar just by five in the evening, daily end hour for receiving RTI act requests.

Shreeja could not help but enquire about meeting detectives on duty. The mail office reluctantly guided her to the detective department.

From desk to desk she asked for information on both the rape spree and begging ring. She got some answers from Sub-inspector Somlata Kundu. She sent Shreeja to her colleague Shiuli Pal at the Missing Persons squad.

Shiuli Pal beamed to Shreeja's encounter with beggars. She opened some logs and advised, "If possible lodge a police complaint at Maidan Police Station about beggars begging on the street."

Shreeja protested, "I had no intention to get a poor misguided woman arrested."

Shiuli suggested, "Mention begging rings. Claim the woman to be a victim. Mention details of your conversation with her as you've done with me. Even mention your meeting with me. And my advice."

Shreeja was listening. Hence, Shiuli continued, "They'll give the diary number; convey it to me by a letter, along with a copy of your complaint to Maidan Police Station. Give me a copy of the letter attached with a copy of your complaint to Maidan Police Station and, also, a copy of the receipt details of my office. To help me start immediately."

Shreeja was still listening. Shiuli Pal stood up, opened a cabinet, and brought a few files. Opening one of them, she showed a picture of a girl, aged around ten to twelve, and explained, “This is Anamita Das. Missing over fifteen years. She had turned twenty-five last spring, if alive. We’re still clueless. There are a few like this.”

She pointed to other files and continued, “Jayati Sinha, Jayeeta Ray, Millie Majumder, Mohul Saha. We’re still looking forward to their return to their respective families.”

Shreeja asked, “None here specializes in begging rings?”

Shiuli replied, “We don’t pursue begging separately. Often street offences are all linked to the same ring, same gang, same cluster of criminals. If we can crack open a piece, we may get a chance to crack the whole thing wide open and get everything resolved. Somlata last year found a victim who was my long-time case. Hence, we share facts and work together. If you stick to it, with or without support of your employer, even without your professional approach, then you shall watch us to see through till the end of this.”

She paused a little and added, “My gut says we’re about to get somewhere with these beggars.”

Shreeja had some epiphany. She had notions of police persons being typical inefficient corrupt public servants. Shiuli made Shreeja believe in the public system and its will.

Shreeja showed the photo she took with the woman and the baby to Shiuli. Shiuli requested Shreeja, “Please email me this photo. I can start pursuing them even before you go to Maidan Police Station.”

Going to office, however, Shreeja wrote how misogyny had been driving the police force and turned its women into ineffective liars protecting its secrets, hiding information from the public. She emphasized that the only secret happened to be inefficacy, amounting to doing nothing for the victims of a misogynistic society. She did not have much information to deliver. She must wait another week for getting responses to her RTI act query. Thus, she could all write about ugly things she imagined of sub-inspector Manidipa Mitra.

Later, at night, at the watering hole Saurabh caught up, "What's about the beggars?"

Shreeja shared everything she encountered till Shiuli Pal's advice. Because both Saurabh and Shreeja knew that every sensation dies after some time. They knew, in a month or two, current rape spree sensation would take a back seat. News cycle would be fed with some new sensations and gradually would delve in indulging the one most enjoyed by the consumers.

Saurabh and Shreeja chalked out a plan for their beggar story. They needed something to survive, first for their soul, then for feeding the news cycle, though with a portion of their soul, as usual. They would make it a money churning game, probably. Until then they would keep digging the truth.

CHAPTER FOUR

Fact Shortage

Months later, Shiuli texted Shreeja to meet immediately. Shreeja rushed to Shiuli's office.

Shiuli said, "The beggar woman you've photographed has resemblances with one of our missing cases, Mohul Saha. Bone structure of her face is a match, but facial features like the shape of eyes, nose, lips, chin are much different. We need her DNA."

Shreeja was perplexed, "What can I do in this matter?"

Shiuli explained, "Simply, you've to collect her DNA. You already have a connection with her. Just take her to a tea stall. Made her eat something. Drink something. We'll bring the plates and glasses and shall collect DNA samples. Our people will be around."

Independence Day had long passed. Even the Puja had passed. Usual route was open. Yet Shreeja got down from the bus at PG hospital stoppage. She walked along the western boundary wall of Rabindrasadan. She did not find the woman.

After two weeks of endeavor, Shreeja spotted the woman along the southern flank of Rabindrasadan. She asked, "Remember me?"

The woman was bewildered, and replied, "No."

Shreeja sought for her child of the day and located a girl, a toddler. She took the toddler in her arms, then cautiously asked, "Is she yours?"

The woman said, "No. my sister's. She died last month. I have taken the orphan in. I must feed her."

Shreeja utilized the opportunity. She took them to Rabindrasadan food stall. The woman and the girl ate some, and took some food packed for later. Shreeja did not feel like giving them any money. She smelled deep conspiracy from the woman's changing mushy stories. A busboy took the paper plates and plastic glasses away wearing disposable gloves. Shreeja received a text from Shiuli, "Got the samples."

Later that night she mentioned it to Saurabh. Saurabh wanted to explore his plan to crack this case. With rape spree sensation dying down and in absence of strong sensations, the news cycle was starving for salaciousness. Saurabh and Shreeja presented their begging ring theory in the weekly meeting with Tapaja and Moumita.

Shreeja and Saurabh were not sure if there would be resources to pursue their plan. They expected to be asked to remain tagged along with the Police. Instead, Tapaja asked, "Take some youngsters. Build a team. Try to enter the hornets' nest. But don't get stung."

Moumita alerted, "As much as I understand, the Police is maintaining a cautious discretion, probably to avoid a blow up. My advice is, you should maintain that too. We need results. To feed the news beast. Hence, don't blow up."

These were more than expectations of Shreeja and Saurabh. They interviewed ten people. They appointed three of them. All girls, Trina, Hridi and Pratiti.

CHAPTER FIVE

Fact Finding

Trina took first turn. She watched the woman on the streets around Rabindrasadan, followed her discreetly on the buses.

A van with Shreeja and Hridi followed Trina. If change of shift required, then, it was planned that Saurabh and Pratiti would take up. Trina marked the house in Behala where the woman entered holding a baby.

It was a big house, in a middle-class neighborhood, with gardens and a pond in the back, very unlike the current paradigm. Also, the house did not have electricity.

Next day Hridi appeared at the doorstep of the house to sell home-made phenyl. A man in his sixties, opened the door and denied buying any phenyl. Hridi asked, "Can I get a glass of water?"

The man could not say, "No." He was hesitating to agree. Hridi feigned fainting. The man had no choice but to take her inside the house.

It was dilapidated. As the man went inside leaving Hridi alone in the room, she fixed a microphone on the door frame, hidden behind panes. Those had no bolt, bar, ring; hence cannot be locked from any side.

The man returned with a woman of his age. They found Hridi roaming all around the room. Hridi apologized for fainting but did not drink their water. A child started crying from inside the house, a few more joined. The man and the woman were not seemingly moved by the cries. Hridi said, "Probably you're busy taking care of children. Sorry to bother you. I must leave now."

She almost ran out of the house. As she entered the surveillance van waiting for her a few meters away, by the turn, Shreeja heard that the woman was scolding the man for letting an unknown girl enter their house and leaving her alone in the room. The man fumbled, "She fainted."

The woman scowled, "Your imagination. You can't keep your hands off young women."

Shreeja told Shiuli about this venture. Shiuli was apprehensive about this unlawful surveillance, its inadmissibility in court of law. She hurried to legitimize surveillance based on Hridi's written statement.

Weeks passed. The beggar woman around Rabindrasadan brought a young man to the house. In the evening.

The old man asked the youth, "Remove your clothes. I must see you completely naked."

They confirmed by observing the naked man that he had no ploy but had fallen into their dragnet, like other prey. The old woman was heard instructing, "You can never have a cell phone. You shall never accompany our girls on the streets. You must ask one of us before you go out."

Shiuli texted Shreeja, "DNA is a match. It's Mohul Saha, indeed. Missing over twenty year and alive."

Shreeja shared the development with Saurabh, Moumita and Tapaja. Tapaja reflected, "It can be a long haul."

Moumita suggested, "One of you must listen to them, daily. Shreeja must maintain liaison with the police. Till it becomes presentable, both of you need to work on other assignments. Your girls will be reassigned to other projects."

CHAPTER SIX

Factory Discovery

After a year and half, Shreeja and Saurabh heard a woman venting, "Sujit can fill the bathroom water tank, clean the toilets, clean the rooms and utensils. Yet he's useless."

A man slandered, "Yah, he can't fuck."

Another man added, "He can be fucked. I did it for him. He can be sold."

They heard another man exclaimed, "Even there's a sex market for older effeminate men? Gracious are human sexual choices!"

The woman teased, "Pedophile. You found only little children sexually attractive. Most people don't."

The man teased back, "You don't even find them adorable. All are commodities for you. You just sell them."

The woman proudly pronounced, "So do my girls."

Shreeja texted Shiuli, "They're planning to sell an effeminate man."

Shiuli texted back, "We're waiting for the purchaser to show up. Money changing hands."

Shreeja texted her mind back, "Outrageous. Can you pull it through at the right moment?"

Shiuli emphasized, "I must."

Then she added, "Come sometime."

Shreeja visited Shiuli. Shiuli showed her a few video clips of the house.

Dirty children, crawling, cooing and crying in a dark room. A young man attempted to clean and feed the children. He was beaten to pulp by another man and a woman. He was seen doing other chores.

There was another dark room full of adolescent girls. They were panting, sulking, groaning. Three men were seen there every day, taking shifts, to rape all those girls, in turns. There were pregnant girls aging ten to fifteen. There was footage of babies being put in duffle bags; those bags being loaded on a minivan.

Stopping the visuals, Shiuli asked, "Are you alright, Shreeja?"

Shreeja barely moved her head in negation. She was devastated. After a long silence Shiuli shared, "That young man is our own Assistant Sub-inspector, Sujit Dam. He had been there for more than a year now. They forced him into the rape room, the factory of producing bastard kids by impregnating adolescent girls,. He could not commit rape. Hence, they labelled him effeminate. Raped him."

Shreeja surmised, "The babies born out of these rapes are the begging fixtures. Couple of which I've adored."

Shiuli added, "They are also sold. The kids as small as fitting in duffle bags, till age of fifteen, to different sex and slave markets, globally. All the children in that house are siblings, half-siblings and their descendants. Some DNA samples are linked to three different women. Mohul Saha, Anamita Das, Jayeeta Ray."

Shreeja asked, "Are all these footages and DNA sample collection Dam's handiwork?"

Shiuli agreed, "Yes, of course. He reconnoitered all the rooms and hotspots like the factory, loading dock, warehouse. Then he collected the surveillance hardware in pretense of running grocery store errands. He fixed both online and offline fixtures himself. He dropped offline footage himself at collection points and collected power backups for all installed equipment along with replacement memory sticks. If online transmission and cloud storage fails.... if devices are caught.... But these savages are so backward that they even avoided electricity."

Shreeja amended, "Nope. That can also be their torture method. The darkness and dirt. Discomfort to break the human will. Keeping victims hungry, angry and weak."

Shiuli further informed, "Our sound and video clips gathered that the five girls were kidnapped separately, subjected to systematic rape and production of children. Later Jayati Sinha and Millie Majumder were sold to local prostitution ring. Probably, they were not as cunning and as useful as Mahul Saha. She has become one of the perpetrators, along with the other two. These three girls marked targets, then, cajoled them to the house. As they did with Sujit."

Shiuli concluded, "Sujit has been fitted with a GPS tracker beneath his skin, between ribs. We'll appear at his sale location. You can follow us but that would be too risky. Till then you must keep mum."

CHAPTER SEVEN

Factor Resolved

A week later, Shreeja and Saurabh started running a story of Renuka Banerjee, the notorious human trafficker and her cousin and aide Bhudeb Ganguly, both in their sixties. It mentioned how a Lalbazar detective arrested Renuka Banerjee, how an Assistant Sub-inspector of Police risked his life to rescue several children. The solace was that the entire operation has found three girls from the city, missing over a decade. Renuka and Bhudeb kidnapped these girls in disguise of household help. Bhudeb alone impregnated them. Their children were raped and impregnated, in turn, while kidnapping of other girls continued. With an increased number of children, the duo hired rapists. Babies, boys and girls, born out of kidnapped girls and their female offspring were trafficked overseas. Otherwise, deployed in local prostitution business, in begging, and as aide to further kidnapping.

Shreeja, Saurabh, Tapaja, Moumita all wanted to name Sujit and Shiuli. But Sujit disagreed, "Why would you put a target on my back? I've just done my job."

Shiuli explained, "We're not immune from the temptation of fame. But we've family. Our names, faces should not be publicized. Criminals and their estranged families may identify and can avenge us for estrangement or death of their loved ones."

Later she added, "This' not at all a glorious moment for the force. Two girls are yet to be found. Countless lives had been violated, lost irredeemably, on our watch. We're far from being done."

Shreeja wanted to thank Shiuli but refrained. Instead, she boozed to forget the pain of lost hope, of unknown helpless children lost into the darkest unknown.

Praises Of The Books By Sanhita Mukherjee

Street Facts: A Thriller Illuminating Darker Mysterious Sides of Streets (Kolkata Crime Cosmos Book 1)

This story is very short and succinct consisting of an event which causes a meeting between Shreeja, who finds a lone child crawling on the pavement and a woman who is a street beggar who rents the child from a gang who control the area, a bit like the Peachums in the Threepenny Opera. There is a lovely description of the child and the way they are fascinated by simple things, especially the tendency for very young children to taste things that aren't edible. I remember my son doing this but don't think I have ever read this in a story...although plenty of idiots guide to parenting books mention this trait, both endearing and concerning,of young explorers in life.I

The life of the beggar woman is revealed in a conversation between the two women and the way even begging is controlled by gangs of men who treat women as second class even though they are the ones doing most of the work. In a very short story misogyny in Indian society and the lengths people will go to to survive in poverty, ways we may find morally repugnant but are a necessity. These people are the invisible people that exist in all societies, the ones some may pretend not to see on leaving the supermarket or tram but who are real people and have real needs. Sometimes a connection between human beings is all that people need to make the day a little brighter.

I wanted to read more about these characters and their lives. How, if at all do I here people cover or is it just a chance meeting that reveals a something about t he society they live in. It reminded me of Tolstoy or Dickens, even

Steven King, all of whom create these little vignettes within a longer story, sometimes with little relevance to the story other than the theme...except Steven King who then kills them off.

https://www.amazon.co.uk/product-reviews/B09LZ2XV4P

How to Steal a Pond: A Literary Fiction with Step by Step Lessons on Corruption

This is another look at the daily lives of people struggling to survive, doing their daily jobs, and learning their limits in forcing their agenda. Sometimes the best outcomes do not require violence but rather solid authority.

https://www.amazon.com/product-reviews/B07NKGLBKT

Maternal Might

Indian storyteller Sanhita Mukherjee spins a tale of female empowerment rooted in love for family and children in "Maternal Might." Bangladeshi mother Fatima becomes the family's breadwinner when she accepts a job as a surrogate for the first child of gay Israeli couple, Abel and Joshua. Mukherjee walks us through the characters' moral dilemma as they get involved in novel arrangements that defy societal norms. The story reinforces the power of money and status in creating opportunities that are not readily available to others.

The story is told from a pragmatic point of view: women living in poverty use their bodies in exchange for money so they can provide for their families. Fatima's job is not different from women's work involving taking care of other people's children. Attitudes about parenting meet modern science with the overlay of religious considerations. A Muslim woman has made the economic decision to bear the child of a Jewish couple in Nepal, a predominantly Buddhist country. Mukherjee boldly discusses these dynamics through dialogue.

In its current iteration, the story is a quick read, but it could easily be adapted to long-form prose. We understand the economic necessity of surrogacy for Fatima, and yet, there's much to explore in Abel and Joshua's decision to become parents. There are also plenty of opportunities to delve into the emotional lives of surrogate mothers. The reader is left wanting more, to explore how the decision of engaging in surrogate motherhood – as the birth mother or the expecting parents – affects everyone involved.

https://www.amazon.com/product-reviews/B09GL3HDGK

Sierra Papa Yankee

This author writes with an intimate knowledge of unrest, violence, and struggling in a different culture. His stories draw the reader into the scene. I would really like to read the entire book.

https://www.amazon.com/product-reviews/B09PBYMNM6

Little Abode for Children: A Mystery (American Small Town Mysteries Book 1)

"Little Abode for Children" is Book 1 of the American Small Town Mysteries series, written by Sanhita Mukherjee .... had an interesting storyline and some pretty great detective and police characters, as well a child characters. Little Abode for Children is the program started at a library by a librarian named Teressa for children who were either homeless, abused, or preyed upon by gang members. The lead detective, Nathan, reminded me of a 1940s/1950s Noir book/movie character. His boss, Captain Brown is a woman, because the text says "she". I liked Captain Brown's character because she was straight forward with her questions to the detective. I also liked the little children, Jack and Melissa.

https://www.amazon.com/product-reviews/B09HSQYBN2

Rescuing the Realm: A Fairytale (Banglish Fairy Tales Book 1)

I liked this story because it depicted the way that one brave person can change the future. A young girl who is low born, Pinky, uses her power to help her people.

https://www.amazon.co.uk/product-reviews/B09RBHXB8F

About The Author

Starts her days with pots and pans. Then pushes 'Ls' after 'P's. Cooks stories with plots and plans.

Her mystery stories are solved by police detectives and fantasy stories include magic realism, sci-fi and epic world building.

Lives with her husband wherever he lives.

For updates on new releases sign in to her newsletter at : https://www.subscribepage.com/x8x3e1 AND Get a book.

Find Her on -

Goodreads: https://www.goodreads.com/author/dashboard?al_user=93464924-sanhita-mukherjee

Twitter: https://twitter.com/SanhitaMukherj6

Facebook: https://www.facebook.com/WrigglerSanhita2000s

Instagram: https://www.instagram.com/sanhitamukherjee3478/

YouTube: https://www.youtube.com/channel/UClyvXlZvL8Yvq2-NBCGeqKw

Blog : https://projectionofnaught.blogspot.com/

Pinterest: https://in.pinterest.com/tupur004/_saved/

Printed by Libri Plureos GmbH in Hamburg,
Germany